LITTLE

OWL

RESCUE

tiger tales

5 River Road, Suite 128, Wilton, CT 06897
Published in the United States 2022
Originally published in Great Britain 2020
by the Little Tiger Group
Text copyright © 2020 Rachel Delahaye
Inside illustrations copyright © 2020 Jo Anne Davies at Artful
Doodlers
Cover illustration copyright © 2020 Suzie Mason
ISBN-13: 978-1-6643-4011-4
ISBN-10: 1-6643-4011-4
Printed in China
STP/1800/0438/1121
10 9 8 7 6 5 4 3 2 1

www.tigertalesbooks.com

LITTLE
OWL
RESCUE

by Rachel Delahaye

tiger tales

Dedicated to the brilliant planet-friendly
18th Bath Brownies, and to Tiya Constantine,
who loves trees
—Rachel

CONTENTS

The Flying Swings

"Isn't this exciting?" Callie shouted over the whirs and cheers. "I love the fair!"

"Me, too," Gabriel said, handing her his raspberry slushie to taste. Callie slurped it and stuck her tongue out. It was stained a bright blue. Gabriel laughed. "You haven't changed a bit, Callie!"

Gabriel was Callie's oldest friend—they'd known each other since they were toddlers. He and his family had moved to France three years ago, but they were back for a few days to visit friends. As a treat, Callie and Gabriel had been allowed to go to the Big Fun Carnival at night! Going at night was extra special because against the darkening sky, the fair looked magical with all its flashing lights, like a giant spaceship.

Callie was full of soda and cotton candy and was happy just to walk around, watching the rides and the faces of the people on them. But Gabriel had other ideas.

"I spy the flying swings!" he said. "Let's go!"

"I'm not sure," Callie said. "I think I've eaten too much to go spinning around."

"Come on. It looks like so much fun!" urged Gabriel. "I have a packet of rainbow glow sticks. We can wave them in the air. It'll be *très cool!*"

He gave her a handful of the clear tubes that would glow neon as soon as they were snapped. Callie agreed that

3

waving rainbow wands high up in the
air would indeed be very cool—or *très
cool*, like Gabriel said. She loved the
way French words crept into his English
language sometimes.

"All right. But I'm warning you, I
might throw up!"

"Only babies throw up. Let's go!"
laughed Gabriel.

Callie didn't usually like heights, but
after her recent adventures of helping
baby animals in the wild, Callie thought
the flying swings would probably be
easy-peasy. And if it made Gabriel
happy, then she would be brave. She
was surprised by how adventurous and
confident he had become. When they
were little, he had been shy and scared
of a lot of things on the playground,

even the slide! While the other kids
played on the monkey bars, he was
happy to play Callie's games of Vet
Hospital instead, even though Callie
always insisted on being the vet. Gabriel
might have changed, but she hadn't—
she still wanted to be a vet!

Callie and Gabriel sat in a seat that
dangled from chains attached to a tall
metal pole. It was just like a regular
swing, except for the safety bar that the
ride operator lowered onto their laps to
keep them from falling out. When the
seats were full, the music started, and
the ride began to turn. It made Callie's
heart flutter. They were so high and
away from the lights of the fair below, it
suddenly seemed scarily dark....

"Here we go!" Gabriel said, kicking

his feet excitedly, rocking the swing.

The seats began to spin faster and faster and then flew out sideways, away from the central pillar that was rising into the air, lifting the swings higher. Callie gasped as the ground dropped away beneath them, and she gripped the safety bar.

"No need to do that," Gabriel said, grinning from ear to ear. "Do this!"

Callie gasped again as Gabriel stretched out his arms as if he were a bird swooping through the sky.

"Are you a *poule mouillée*?" Gabriel asked.

"A what?"

"A *poule mouillée*—it means wet chicken. A scaredy-cat!"

"I am definitely not a wet chicken!"

Callie said. To show him, she let go of
the bar and stretched out her arms even
wider than he did.

"Now you're a flying wet chicken,"
Gabriel laughed.

Callie felt more like an eagle than a
chicken! She ignored her friend's teasing
and enjoyed the moment. Below her
dangling feet, lights twinkled like glitter,
and the people wandering through the
fair looked as small as ants.

Straight ahead, Callie could see
streetlights marking the crisscrossing
streets of the town and beyond that
farms and fields, all gray green in the
dusky light. It looked like a living
map.

*Wouldn't it be incredible to see the world
from this high every day?* Callie thought.

Then, out of nowhere, gusts of wind brought huge gray clouds toward them. The damp fog wrapped around everything like thick cotton candy, and soon Callie could no longer see her living map or even her hands in front of her face. Or Gabriel next to her.

"Gabriel?"

Callie wanted him to call her a wet chicken and tell her that everything was okay, but there was no answer.

"Don't panic, Catalina," she said to herself sternly, using her full name just as her mom would. "It's only a cloud. It will pass in a minute. The ride will end soon."

But the cloud didn't pass, and the spinning didn't slow down. In fact, it sped up. Callie was whisked around and around. She reached out for Gabriel, but he had disappeared.... Oh, no!

She tried to call for help, but the wind whipped the words from her mouth. She squeezed her eyes shut and hoped the ride would stop.

Then suddenly, it did.

Callie was standing still, with solid ground beneath her feet. She waited for the dizziness to disappear and carefully opened her eyes. The cloud had cleared, revealing a beautiful royal-blue sky underlined by an orange glow, where the sun had just dipped below the horizon.

But the sun set hours ago, Callie puzzled. *And where's the carnival, the noise, the people?*

They were all gone, and Callie got the feeling that she was a long, long way from home.

The Night Glider

Callie looked around. She was standing on a raised dusty road, which sloped on each side into crop fields below. Except for the occasional clump of trees, she couldn't see anything else—just miles and miles of farmland—and there was nothing to tell her where she was. Callie knew from experience that she could be anywhere on Earth.

She had been transported before, finding herself in new countries and environments, and each time it meant one thing: a young animal needed her help.

Where she had been brought to this time, she had no idea, and except for the flies that buzzed around her, there were no animals to be seen.

"I know you're out there somewhere," Callie said out loud. "Don't worry. I'll find you!"

It was easy to say, but Callie didn't know where to start looking. She turned in circles, wondering which way to walk. In every direction, she saw the same thing: yellowing crops in neat rows, separated by little pathways, all rose-tinted by the beautiful apricot sunset. But then, over there, two fields up.... What was that?

Something large and square was
sparkling in the last of the Sun's rays. It
didn't look like an animal, but it could
be a hut or a signpost. There was only
one way to find out.

Callie ran down the dusty track and
along two fields, then turned into the
field where she'd seen the object. But as

soon as she ran down the slope toward it, she lost sight of everything. The crops now towered over her head. The plants had long stalks, with peeling leaves and solid pods. They looked familiar, but Callie's mind was focused on locating the shiny object she'd seen. Now that her view was blocked, she had to hope that her sense of direction was good. She ran down a path between the rows, occasionally battling through clumps of the plants to get to the next path across, closer to where she wanted to be.

She was tired and about to give up when suddenly she saw it. Parked in the middle of the field was a huge white tractor. Her heart sank a little when she saw that there was no one inside. No one who could tell her where she was and what animals could be found in the area. But there was writing on the side in swirly red letters.

"King O' Corn, Skyville, Texas." Callie nodded her head. "I'm in Texas! And that must be corn!"

Fresh corn on the cob was one of the yummiest things ever. Her mother always gave them to her cooked, but sometimes Callie ate them raw. She loved how the sweet kernels popped in her mouth.... Something in the distance caught her eye. A small white bird with huge wings was flying toward her. Even in the dying light, it looked dazzling as it glided silently through the warm air. An owl. Definitely an owl. And as it came closer, Callie recognized the telltale heart-shaped face.

"A barn owl," Callie whispered as it flew over her head. "A beautiful barn owl."

She watched the owl swoop closer. It was barely flapping its wings, and yet it traveled quickly and smoothly. A bird of prey expert named Mr. Howell had once visited Callie's school. He had brought falcons, hawks, and owls of all sizes that had been trained to come when he called. They had been incredible—so alert, with their staring eyes and their heads turning at the slightest sound. Callie had been transfixed by the barn owl. The sleek feathers on his underside had been brilliant-white, and they had fanned out in a heart shape as perfect as a cookie cutter on his face.

The owl was
gliding low
over the field,
right above her.
It had a little field
mouse in its claws, and
as it continued overhead, Callie could
see its jet-black marble eyes and flat,
pointy beak.

That's strange, Callie thought. *Why
would it come so close to me? It's not like
I'm small enough to eat, and it has prey
already—a little mouse. Why didn't the
owl gobble up the mouse?*

"You have owlets that need feeding!"
Callie exclaimed to the sky. "That's why
you didn't eat the mouse. Maybe your
babies need my help.... Well, that's fine
by me. If I get to see a bunch of barn

owls, I think I'm going to enjoy being here in Skyville, Texas!"

Callie wasn't sure if she was right, but the beautiful barn owl was the only animal she'd seen since she'd arrived. It was definitely worth investigating. *Follow that owl!* She ran as fast as she could along the path and back toward the dusty road, where she would be higher up and have a better view.

As she ran, she broke out in a sweat. The air was thick with heat and dust; the ground beneath her was dry and cracked. It was still warm now—the day must have been scorching hot. That beautiful yellow sunset was probably a relief for the animals and the farmers— the air would be turning cooler, just for a while.

I'd be nocturnal, too, if I lived in such a hot place! Callie thought.

And as she stepped back up onto the track, she saw it. The white owl. It looked like nothing more than a scrap of paper on the breeze as it flapped toward a cluster of trees in the distance. Callie watched as it circled a while, almost as if it were waiting for her, before disappearing into the woods.

King O' Corn

Callie ran down the track and into the
next cornfield, disappearing once again
between the rows of towering corn.
After the endless scratch and dust of
the dry corn leaves, Callie was looking
forward to being in the greener, shadier
woods and couldn't wait to explore. She
was sure the owl was leading her there
for a reason.

But as soon as she broke through the
corn thicket next to the woods, she came

upon a strange sight. There was bright orange sawdust all over the forest floor, and tree stumps—maybe a hundred of them—that looked like they had been freshly cut. Though the light was dim, she could see that farther into the woods, where the trees became thicker, there were more stumps and newly fallen trees lying on the ground. Then she saw the sign.

King O' Corn Farm
Clearing in progress for expansion
of crop fields. For more information
contact Herman.

They were chopping down the woods to grow more corn!
Surely no animals would still be living

here with the noise of the chainsaws and the tree cutters coming and going with their trucks! Maybe the owl hadn't entered the woods at all but had flown right through them and out the other side.

Just then, Callie heard a hoot. It came from somewhere in the trees.

"Or maybe you're hanging on to your home until the end," she said anxiously. "Don't worry; I'm coming."

Tripping on scattered branches and logs in the hazy light, Callie crept into the woods. She looked all around for signs of the barn owl or any other creatures that might be in trouble. Then she spotted it, straight ahead. The white bird, much smaller now, with its wings tucked back in place, was pacing the ground by a tree stump, the mouse dangling in its beak.

Maybe her nest was in the tree that was chopped down! Callie thought. *That's why she's looking confused.*

Callie began to panic. She was certain that the owl was a mother, and the mouse was a meal for her babies. So where were they now? Callie wanted to run to the mother owl and comfort it, but she stopped herself.

"Animals don't always feel like we do, and all vets know you should watch an animal first before doing anything."

Watching an animal to see how it behaved was the best way to find out the bigger picture. Maybe this owl didn't need her help after all. Then it would be terrible to scare her away!

Callie ducked behind a tree stump and watched, blinking in the fading light, not

wanting to miss a thing. For a while,
nothing happened—the owl just paced,
but suddenly, three smaller owls
staggered into the open from behind a
fallen tree. The nest must have crashed to
the ground! Their bright white feathers
were a little ruffled, but they didn't seem
to be hurt. Maybe the surrounding trees
had cushioned their fall. Everything was
fine!

Thank goodness I didn't act too quickly, Callie thought. *And what a treat to be able to see a mother with her babies.*

This owl family was fine, which meant Callie would have to look elsewhere for the animal that needed her help. Right now, though, she would stay and watch what this pretty owl family did next.

The owl mother shared the mouse between the owlets. They squabbled over it—hopping around, flapping their wings, and making such a fuss that Callie could hardly see what was going on! All she knew was that they gobbled down the mouse in seconds. They must have been starving. Callie wondered how long it had been since they last ate. She remembered Mr.

Howell telling them that mother barn
owls weren't very good parents—
they often disappeared for days, and
sometimes slept in another nest, away
from their owlets. Maybe she hadn't
fed them in a while. *Or maybe,* Callie
thought, looking at the tree stumps, *all
the farming has made it harder to find
food.*

Suddenly, without warning, the
mother launched herself off into the
woods. Her flight was totally silent,
and Callie wouldn't have noticed her
leave if she hadn't turned at the right
moment. Although it might be normal
behavior for a mother owl, Callie was
worried. Owlets on the ground could
be food for snakes or other creatures....

Phew! The mother had returned. But

she didn't land. She circled over the owlets below.

There was a frantic beating of wings and then one, two of the owlets made it off the ground and into the air, where they flapped like crazy. They were up for a few seconds before they landed awkwardly and off balance, like planes on a windy day. Then the mother flew off again and the two owlets tried once more, stretching out their wings this time, looking more confident and flying—actually flying! Without any hesitation, they followed after their mother, which left just one.

The owlet on the ground hopped into the air, testing its wings each time its feet were off the ground. But it wasn't getting the hang of it. Callie

looked in the direction of the owls'
flight, but there was no flash of white
in the dark tree canopy. They weren't
circling back. They were gone.

"The mother will return," Callie said to herself. "She probably just left to find a new nest."

As the owlet kept trying to fly, and each time landing with a graceless tumble on the ground, Callie wanted more than anything to pick it up and give it a hug. But she knew the owlet would learn to fly eventually, and she shouldn't get in the way. Not unless something terrible was about to happen.

4

Horn and Claws

Callie didn't know how long she had
waited for the mother to return, but it
was now nighttime, and some parts of
the woods were in total darkness. She
wouldn't have been able to see anything
at all if it weren't for the moonbeams
that made their way through the gaps
in the trees. A shaft of moonlight
shone through a section where the tree
chopping had created a big hole in the
canopy, and it cast a light on the baby

owl. The poor thing had grown tired of trying to fly and now stood perfectly still, like a large white pebble.

What should I do? What should I do? Callie's mind turned over and over, wondering if she should pick up the bird. It was now clear that the owlet had been abandoned. She wouldn't be doing it any harm.

The first thing she had to do was introduce herself. If she just ran over and picked up the owlet, it could damage a wing trying to get away or even die of fright. She had to be gentle but confident, because she knew that animals sensed if you were nervous, and that could make them nervous, too.

Callie straightened up from her crouched position behind the tree stump so she could be seen. But still the owlet didn't move. Maybe it was too scared to look around.

"Hey, little one," Callie said softly. "I'm not going to hurt you."

She began to walk forward slowly, placing each foot down very carefully so she wouldn't trip on the uneven ground. The owlet was startled by the movement and tried to fly away. It managed to get up onto the tree stump, and then it froze. Something had caught its eye.

Callie looked up. There, shooting through a shaft of moonlight, she saw a bird. An owl!

"Is that your mother? So she did come back for you!"

Callie immediately started to move away, not wanting to alarm the mother.

If she thought it was too dangerous to land, she might fly off again and never return. Although Callie knew that barn owl parents weren't very protective, maybe this owl was different.

But as the owl flew through another patch of light, Callie noticed that it wasn't beige and white; it was varying shades of brown. It wasn't a barn owl.

As the bird swooped closer, Callie saw it had strange tufty feathers on its head. They looked almost like pointy cat ears or horns. A large tail fanned out behind it. Its eyes were yellow and piercing.

"A great horned owl!" Callie gasped.

They were easy to identify because of their remarkable "horns." And they were so vicious, Mr. Howell had explained in a funny voice, that they would eat anything they could get their claws into. Even other birds.

Callie saw the intensity on its face as it drew near. Then its stumpy legs came down—huge, four-toed talons splayed out on each foot. It was then that Callie realized the horned owl was not planning to land.

It was after the baby owl!

If there was a time to get involved, it was definitely now. Shouting loudly to disturb the horned owl's concentration, Callie ran forward and grabbed the baby barn owl. She held it tightly against her chest and turned her back just in time. The attacker's strong wings whipped across her. Callie braced herself for the scratch of razor-sharp talons or the dagger of a beak, but it never came. Realizing that its prey had been stolen, it was already flying away.

"That was so close," Callie said aloud. She was panting, her heart beating fast with the adrenalin. "Thank goodness I was here, or you might have been...."

She trailed off, not wanting to think about what might have happened to the owlet, and then she realized something.

"A-ha!" she said, smiling. "It's you. *You're* the reason I'm here, aren't you?"

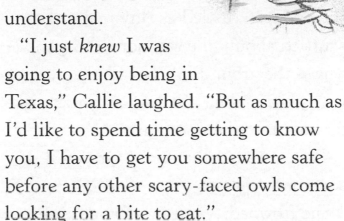

The owlet circled its head as if it were trying to understand.

"I just *knew* I was going to enjoy being in Texas," Callie laughed. "But as much as I'd like to spend time getting to know you, I have to get you somewhere safe before any other scary-faced owls come looking for a bite to eat."

Callie took the cardigan she'd tied around her waist and wrapped the owlet in it. "I'm not sure where to start, but one thing's for sure—I can't leave you here alone. We'll have to do this together."

Callie stared into the woods, wondering what to do. There weren't any gliding barn owls to show her the way. There was no movement at all, except for on the forest floor, where the odd leaf rustled as tiny mammals scuttled about. She saw something move across the ground in front of them, lit up by the moon. It darted as quickly as it could into the undergrowth.

"Yes, run!" Callie said. "Or you'll be someone's dinner."

She frowned. With more and more trees disappearing every day, soon there would be nowhere for these creatures to hide. And maybe nowhere for the owls to live, either. With a big sigh, Callie looked down into the heart-shaped face of the baby barn owl.

"Before we worry about the future, we need to think what to do right now."

Will You Be My Friend?

The woods were so dark that Callie realized she'd never be able to find the barn owl's nest. She could hardly see a few feet ahead, let alone a hole in a tree trunk.

"This rescue mission isn't going to be completed tonight, that's for sure!" she said. "We'll have to wait until dawn. But in the meantime, let's take a look at you."

Callie wanted to check that the little owl hadn't been damaged in her rush to save it. She'd tried to be gentle, but handling wildlife could be tricky—and birds had such tiny bones, which could easily break under too much pressure. She just hoped that when she'd scooped up the owlet, she hadn't been too rough. It had all happened so quickly.

There was more moonlight out in the open, so Callie carried her precious bundle back toward the cornfield. By the edge of the crops, she crouched down and unwrapped her cardigan, revealing the little bird inside.

It was shivering a little. Maybe with fear.

"Hello," Callie said softly. "My name is Callie, and I'm going to do everything I can to help you. I want to be a vet when I grow up, so I've read plenty of books about animals and watched a bunch of TV programs, too. I'd love to be your friend!"

She didn't know if it was possible to form a friendly bond with a bird, but she hoped her calm voice would soothe the little owl. It seemed to work. The owlet looked up at her and twisted its head to one side as if to say hello.

"If we're going to spend some time together, I should give you a name. I can't just call you owl.... Hmmm, let's see." Although Callie loved all animals, she didn't know much about owls—just what Mr. Howell had taught them, which didn't include figuring out whether they were boys or girls. Callie decided it didn't really matter, but she had a feeling the owl was a girl. She looked down at the pretty little face with its perfect cookie-cutter heart shape.

"That's it! You can be Cookie!"

Cookie hopped around, and Callie sat back and watched for any awkward movements or limping to show that she was injured. But the owlet seemed fine. More than fine! She jumped backward and forward as if she were playing hopscotch.

"There's nothing wrong with you!" Callie said.

Cookie had stopped shivering and seemed to be enjoying herself.

Callie noticed that while the owl had mainly white plumage, the feathers on the tops of her wings and at the edges of her face were a light brown color. She couldn't be very young, because in the video of nesting barn owls they had watched at school, the really young ones were strange-looking things—scrawny, white and fluffy, like startled balls of cotton wool!

Cookie was a beautiful shape. Solid and smooth. If only Callie could remember more of the information from Mr. Howell's video.... Oh, yes! It said that by the age of eight or nine weeks, they'd have tried flying, and from then on they got better and better at it, but they still lived in their nest for months.

"So you're at least two months old,"

Callie said, watching Cookie as she
extended her wings and flapped a little.
The owlet ran back toward Callie, wings
still extended as if she were pretending
to be an airplane! The feathery tips
brushed against Callie's face.

"You may not be quite as advanced as
your siblings, but you're not far behind.
You need to catch up quickly, though,"
Callie added, remembering something
else Mr. Howell had said. *If a baby
barn owl can't get back into the nest, it's
abandoned.* This had made Callie sad at
the time, and now that she had a real-
life abandoned owlet in front of her, it
was even more upsetting.

"That's what we're going to do," Callie
said with determination. "We're going to
get you flying, so wherever your nest is,

you can find it. Even if I can't. Let's start now—there's no time to lose!"

Callie didn't know how to teach an owl how to fly, but she had to try.

Cookie was hopping and flapping on the small strip of land in front of them, between the tree stumps at the edge of the woods and the tall crops in the cornfield. Callie crouched and leaned forward to where the little owl had stopped for a moment and was folding in one of her wings.

Callie tied her cardigan back around her waist and wrapped her hands around Cookie's soft body, lifting her off the ground just a little. Then she shuffled her hands so they were supporting Cookie's feet and noticed immediately how sharp those little talons were. Ignoring the scratching sensation, Callie looked into Cookie's dark eyes. They were like two little coals in the snow.

"I'm going to throw you into the air, okay? Then flap as hard as you can. Don't worry —if you fall, you're not far from the ground."

Callie raised her hands up and down so that Cookie could get used to the movement. Just as she had hoped, the owlet's reaction was to lift her wings to get her balance.

"Excellent, Cookie! Great job. Now for the real thing. Ready, set … go!"

Callie jerked her hands upward, and the little owl released her claws and let go. She flapped wildly in the air just in front of Callie's face.

"Yes, Cookie! You're doing it!"

The owlet was only in the air for a moment, but she didn't fall down. Instead, she landed on Callie's outstretched hand and quickly hopped up her wrist and along her arm. Before Callie knew what was going on, Cookie had folded in her wings and was happily perched on Callie's shoulder.

Callie giggled. "Well, that settles it. We're definitely friends now!"

48

To Catch a Mouse

The night air was fragrant with earthy smells and it was still warm, even though the sun had gone down a long time ago. Callie breathed in deeply and smiled. *I'll never forget this moment,* she thought. Standing in a cornfield in Texas with a baby owl roosting on your shoulder didn't happen every day!

Callie could feel the weight of Cookie and the light grip of her talons over her shoulder. Whenever Cookie shuffled, her

wing feathers brushed Callie's cheeks, and
Callie had to try so hard not to laugh in
case she scared the little owl—but it was
Cookie who suddenly startled Callie....

Psssh-cheee. Psssh-cheee.

What a strange noise. It sounded like a
snore and a jet of steam, and it was really
loud, right in Callie's ear!

Psssh-cheee. Psssh-cheee.

Callie decided that Cookie must be so
comfortable on her shoulder that she'd
fallen asleep. The snoring was cute, but
now wasn't the time to be resting. Only
when Cookie had learned to fly could
either of them take a break.

"Come on, Cookie," Callie coaxed.
"Back to work now. If we don't get you in
the air soon, you might never find your
family."

Callie reached her hand across her body and carefully dislodged the owl, expecting it to wake up. Carefully, she pulled Cookie down and brought her other hand up to support the sleeping owlet, cradling it in her arms.

Only Cookie wasn't asleep.

Psssh-cheee. Psssh-cheee.

Her little dark eyes were wide open, and with every odd screech, she opened and closed her mouth. No, not a sleeping sound after all. Then what was it? Cookie let out a super loud rasp but kept her mouth wide open, making her look more like a brand-new baby than a fledgling.

"A-ha! I know what you want," Callie said. "Food! You didn't get any of the mouse, did you?"

Callie remembered the owlets squabbling over the mouse that the mother had dropped. Maybe it was because they weren't used to eating outside of the nest, or maybe the stronger ones were just looking after themselves, but Cookie hadn't managed to get her beak anywhere close. Now she was hungry.

What do barn owls eat? Callie asked herself. She thought hard, trying to recall Mr. Howell's talk. *Ugh, why didn't I listen more carefully to the most important part?* Usually she paid close attention, but this time, she hadn't been able to stop staring at the majestic birds he'd brought with him! Knowing an animal's diet was key to providing it with good care, and Callie was annoyed with herself. But it wouldn't help to dwell on what she couldn't remember; she had to use her common sense.

Obviously, owls ate mice—but what about insects or worms, which would be much easier to catch? Callie couldn't be sure. Her best friend, Ella, had once tried to feed cheese to a baby mouse she had found on the pavement, and it didn't end well. It was never a good idea to guess. It would have to be a mouse, Callie decided. It was the only thing she was certain of. She didn't know if she could kill another creature, even if it was part of nature's cycle, but she would worry about that when the time came. First, she had to find a mouse!

"Your clever mother caught one in a cornfield," Callie said, placing Cookie back on her shoulder. "So hold on tight, because that's where we're going."

As Callie stepped between the rows of corn, the scraggy leaves brushed against her, and Cookie clung tighter, nuzzling into Callie's hair for protection. Here the corn was fat and ready. Callie could see the cobs in the moonlight clinging to the tall stems, each with a tuft of fibers sprouting from the top like hair. She would have loved to crunch into one of those sweet pods, but she probably shouldn't take from the farmer's crop, and besides, it was unfair to eat while Cookie was so hungry. She had to help this young animal in need before she could think about herself.

Callie continued walking deep into the field, her eyes on the rows of corn on either side of her path. But there was no sign of a mouse or anything other than the winged insects and moths that flittered against her face. Callie couldn't give up trying.

The rustling of the corn plants as she brushed by them sounded loud in the stillness of the night. It was only when Callie stopped to wipe the sweat from her brow that she noticed the difference. When she wasn't moving, it was so quiet. Of course! If there was any chance of catching a mouse, then marching noisily through the field was going to ruin it. Callie remembered how the mother barn owl had swooped over the corn—she was perfectly silent.

"You should always learn from animals," Callie muttered to herself, shaking her head. "How could I forget such an important lesson? Cookie, from now on we're going to have to be stealthy."

Callie put her foot forward, but immediately the plants swooshed and scratched. It was no good. They would have to be absolutely still. Maybe Cookie would have a better chance on her own.

"I just make a lot of noise and scare everything away. Let's see how you do, shall we?" Callie said, taking Cookie from her shoulder and placing her on the ground. They both stood quietly, listening for the teeniest of crunches and rustles among the corn.

Then Cookie heard something. Her head twisted sideways, locating the sound.

Go on, Cookie, Callie willed. *Find your dinner!*

Cookie hopped off the path, into the crops and out of sight. Callie didn't know what to do. If she didn't follow, she might lose Cookie. But if she did follow, she'd create too much noise....

Suddenly, there was a noise louder than any Callie could make. It roared like a beast, with a crackle like a bonfire. If there had been any mice nearby, they'd have run away. Callie started to think that maybe she should, too.

Because whatever it was, it sounded angry.

The Beast

"Cookie! Cookie!" Callie cried urgently. "We have to go. Now!"

Growling, roaring, crackling. Was it a herd of angry bulls stampeding through the crops? Callie had no idea what was making the noise, only that it was getting closer.

She desperately wanted to run.

"Cookie!" she called again, but her voice was drowned out by the sound, and there was no sign of the little owl. Cookie had hopped deep into the undergrowth.

Callie couldn't leave without her. But she couldn't just stand there, either.

To avoid danger, I need to see what I'm dealing with, she thought.

Callie jumped as high as she could, over and over again, trying to see above the tall corn plants. But no matter how hard she tried, she couldn't see anything except the tips of the corn in the moonlight and the dark sky above.

"Ugh!" she shouted in frustration. There was only one thing left to do— head back to the dusty track and get a clearer view. But that meant leaving Cookie.

"If I can't see what's coming until it's too late, then Cookie won't have any chance at all," Callie convinced herself.

She dropped her cardigan on the path so she could find her way back to the exact spot she had last seen Cookie and ran back toward the track. The roaring continued, and Callie found herself short of breath from running in the sticky, warm air, and also from fear. She felt as if she were being hunted.

Don't be silly, Callie. Whatever it is can't see you! she told herself.

It was easy to fear what you didn't

know, and if you were unsure, sometimes it was better to slow down and figure out what it *wasn't*. And it probably *wasn't* angry bulls, because as far as Callie could tell, there were only cornfields for miles, not cattle farms. There had to be a simple explanation.

As Callie ran up the slope to the dusty track, she saw it.

In the distance, vast beams of light swept over the field, making the corn look like skinny dancing ghosts. Behind them were giant machines—a row of them with huge rotating arms, each with blades sharp enough to cut down anything in their path. Combine harvesters. They were harvesting the corn!

Cut down anything in their path....

"Oh, no! Cookie!" Callie yelled, speeding back down into the field.

She ran in a blind panic, tripping over the cardigan she'd left as a marker. Her knee hit the ground with a thwack, and she cried out in pain. But there was no time to worry about her own injuries— if she didn't get to Cookie in time, she'd have failed in her mission to rescue and protect animals in need. And that would cause her much more pain than a scratched knee. Callie snatched up her cardigan and got to her feet, trying to hear any sound of Cookie hopping around in the corn, but the approaching harvesters were even noisier than before, and it was impossible.

"Cookie!" she cried as loud as she could.

Stepping off the path and pushing her way through the corn, Callie ignored the discomfort of the scratchy leaves and paper-dry stalks that nicked at the skin on her legs and face. She shouted for the little owl as the machines advanced, their long light beams now dancing on the corn around her. It wouldn't be long until the harvesters were right there, cutting up the corn, shredding the stalks and destroying everything at her feet.

Callie pushed on, her nose full of the dust that billowed from the shredded crops in clouds. When the dust settled, it covered everything in a fine, itchy powder. But there was no time to wipe it away. With every second, the harvesters were getting closer, and then—Cookie!

Just ahead of her, the owlet was in half flight—flapping in the air before falling back down again.

"It's not the time for flying practice now!" Callie shouted. "Cookie, come back!"

But whether Cookie was chasing a mouse or enjoying the feeling of being in the air, she clearly wasn't ready to stop. Callie quickened her step in an effort to catch up with her feathered friend. She lost sight of the owl for a moment, and then suddenly Cookie was lit up—a luminous white bird in the harvesters' high-beam headlights.

They were here. Just feet away. The machines growled deafeningly, and the crunch of the crops between their blades sent a shiver of terror down Callie's spine.

"Cookie, please!" she shouted,

running toward the owl and right up to
the mouths of the harvesters that were
quickly eating up the space between
them.

Callie lunged forward to catch Cookie,
but the owl flapped and caught the
air beneath her wings, sending her up
and over the next row of corn. Callie
followed in terror, her breath caught
in her throat. The lights were now
dazzling, blinding her if she looked at
them straight on. She needed to get out
of there fast! But not without Cookie.
Callie pushed through to the next
row of corn and there, in a cloud of
brilliantly lit dust particles, Cookie hung
above the corn, wings fully extended. It
was now or never.

Using all her strength, Callie leaped

up and snatched Cookie from the air.

She fell to the ground with a thud. Ouch! But it didn't matter. She had the owl, and now they needed to run. With the growling, crunching noise following just behind, Callie sprinted as fast as her tired legs would carry her. She ran back toward the track, the harvesters still so close that their beams lit the way ahead of her. Callie's ears were full of the jarring sound.

She turned to see how far behind the machines were, and that's when she tripped.

Glow in the Dark

Callie yelled at them to stop but it was no good. In the cabins of the harvesters, the drivers were busy checking switches and dials. They weren't looking down, so they couldn't see the little girl clutching a tiny owl, lying in the gloom of the alley between the corn. Callie squeezed her eyes tightly … and everything went black.

She opened her eyes and blinked at the sudden darkness around her. The lights were gone. When her eyes adjusted, she saw that the harvesters had swung around and were heading back the other way, rumbling across the cut corn toward the farm.

Callie lay flat on her back, her heart pounding, overcome with relief. Then she started to laugh. She laughed and laughed and couldn't stop. Cookie hopped onto her tummy and tried to look into her face, curious about the funny noise she was making. This only made Callie giggle more, and Cookie dug her claws in to keep her balance as Callie's tummy jiggled with laughter. That hurt enough to make her stop.

"When I realized I'd be rescuing a little owl, I had no idea it would be quite this dangerous!" Callie said, sitting up and taking Cookie in her arms. "You must be the most troublesome owlet in all of Texas. Maybe even all of the United States!"

Callie placed Cookie on the ground and stood up to brush herself off. She was covered in dust and flecks of corn, and probably bruises, too, although it was too dark to see. *Thank goodness for the moon,* she thought, looking at the white bird at her feet. *Without it, I'd be lost.* Humans are *not* nocturnal animals. She crouched down and held out her arm, as she'd seen Mr. Howell do with his birds of prey.

"Hop up, Cookie," she said. And the owl did. "Good girl! Come on—let's get back to the woods so we're closer to your family. We'll take a short rest and think about what to do next."

Walking back to the tree stumps, Callie felt a gnawing ache in her stomach. Poor Cookie hadn't eaten yet, but how could Callie think clearly with her own tummy rumbling? She set Cookie down on one of the stumps and stepped toward the cornfield, where a few stalks had escaped the harvesters. There on the ground was a fallen pod. The farmer surely wouldn't miss this one. She peeled back the stringy husk to reveal the fresh corn, gleaming like beads in the moonlight.

"Oh, that's so good!" Callie sighed, chomping on the refreshing corn. "I guess that's why they harvest at night, so the corn is cooler and better to store."

She turned to look at Cookie. The little owl was tilting her head as if she were trying to understand Callie's language. A moonbeam revealed her standing patiently, twisting her heart-shaped face from side to side—clockwise, then counterclockwise. But Callie's eyes were quickly drawn to another, darker figure lurking on the ground just behind the stump. Although it was in the shadows, Callie could see it skulking. It was the size of a large cat, but cats didn't have

long, bushy tails like that.... What
was it?

The shape moved around the tree
stump, occasionally lifting itself on its
hind legs to look up. Sniffing, maybe.
Whatever it was, it was interested in
Cookie.... It shuffled around, and then,
hit by another beam of moonlight
through the trees, Callie could see exactly
what it was. It was gray and white, with
black markings across its nose and
eyes—a raccoon!

Callie had seen raccoons in
documentaries about animals. She'd
always thought they looked funny and
sweet, with their big whiskers, bandit-
mask markings, and pointy noses—but
they were often described as pests. They
raided garbage cans and destroyed

everything in their hunt for food. If they got into your house, they could trash it in minutes. They were fierce scavengers and would eat anything. On one program, a woman described how a raccoon attacked her small dog....

Uh-oh. *That's why it was interested in Cookie!*

Without stopping to think about what might happen, Callie ran at the raccoon. "Shoo! Get away!"

But the raccoon didn't move.

"I said get out of here!" Callie shouted. She ran right up to it, ready to nudge it away with her foot if needed. But there was something strange about the furry hunter. It wasn't scared of her, even though she was much bigger. Why wasn't it running away?

The raccoon waited until Callie was standing right in front of it before it turned and lunged at her, making a weird noise—something between a growl and a hiss. Callie saw its eyes like green marbles. Its fangs, too—sharp white points. Quickly, she ran backward and hoped it would follow her, away from Cookie. But the raccoon wasn't going to be tricked that easily.

It started leaping up at the tree stump.

"No!" she yelled. But it didn't make a difference.

Quick, Callie, think of something, she thought to herself. *How can I scare it away?*

Remembering that earlier she had been scared by noises she didn't understand, Callie suddenly had a great idea. She pulled a thin plastic tube out of her pocket.

"We're frightened of what we don't know," she said softly. "So what do you think of this?"

She snapped the tube in three places, which quickly set off a chemical reaction inside it. The glow stick turned red, orange, yellow, green, blue—all the colors of the rainbow—and Callie boldly

stepped
forward,
waving it at
the raccoon
and making
the weirdest
noises she
could think of.

"Bet you haven't
seen one of these before, have you?" she
sang.

The raccoon wasn't so quick to fight
back this time. Instead, it seemed
mesmerized by the wand, and then,
without warning, it scuttled off.

Callie ran toward the little owl and
crouched down. "Oh, Cookie, the
world is a dangerous place when you
don't have a home," she said, suddenly

thinking of her own home, so far away.

Cookie leaped onto her shoulder, nestling once again in her hair.

"Don't worry. I'm not going anywhere. Not until I know you're one hundred percent safe."

Lessons from an Owl

Callie sat down on the stump, looking out at the moonlit field, now empty of corn. She felt just as empty of ideas.

Cookie couldn't fly yet—not very well, anyway. Although she tried, she kept coming down after a few seconds like a kite with no wind. Callie had to get Cookie back to her nest as soon as possible, in case another sneaky raccoon or horned owl came by.

"But how can I help you?" Callie said,

reaching up to touch the owl's tummy feathers. "I can't fly, either, so I'll never be able to find your family or a new nest safely up in the trees."

Callie reached across, took Cookie from her shoulder, and placed the owl on her lap. They sat in silence, listening to the gentle swoosh of the light night breeze in the treetops and the occasional scuttle among the debris of the corn in the field.

Psssh-cheee. Psssh-cheee.

Callie was woken from her worries by that familiar noise. Cookie was hungry.

Psssh-cheee. Psssh-cheee.

"Okay, we can look for food again. But if you want a mouse, you're going to have to hunt for it yourself," Callie said. "One crunch of my feet on that dry grass, and they'll run away. But you can't go far. I'm keeping you in my sights this time."

She set Cookie on the ground. The owl listened intently, twisting her head this way and that way, hearing noises that Callie couldn't. Every rustle, every shuffle—Cookie was listening. Callie marveled at how she could move her head around and side to side in order to hear the noises more clearly. Her big, circular face was like a satellite dish, rotating to get the best signal.

But if Cookie did hear a mouse, she wasn't going to chase it. After only a few seconds, the owl bounced back toward Callie and fluttered clumsily up to her perch on Callie's shoulder.

"I'm not surprised you're scared," Callie soothed. "I would be, too, after everything that's happened."

Callie sat still and allowed herself to think of home. How would she ever get back? She knew from previous adventures that she could only return once the baby animal was safe. But sitting here in the dark, straining to see anything in the gloom, she had no idea how to make Cookie safe. She felt bruised and sore, tired and helpless.

"Come on, Callie, think!" she said to herself crossly. "What would a vet do?"

Callie thought back to the research she
had done into being a vet. One of the first
things she'd learned was that you had to
respect the animal.

"Well, I definitely respect animals," she
said. "More than anything! I could do all
the research in the world, but animals
will always know their environment
better than me...."

Callie jumped up excitedly. "That's it!
You're the teacher!"

Cookie made a funny noise—it
sounded like a little laugh.

Callie giggled. "Miss Cookie, all this
time you've been teaching me how to be
an owl. And finally, I think I've figured
out the most important lesson: listening."

Callie had been nervous about going
back into the woods to find Cookie's

mother. It seemed so pointless when she couldn't see anything. A few steps past the stumps, the moonlit night faded into total darkness. The thought of being in the pitch-black and not being able to see frightened her, but for animals, it wasn't such a big deal. Not if they used their other senses. Callie thought of Cookie's stillness when listening and how she tried to locate the sound by turning her head....

With Cookie tucked into her neck, Callie would be able to feel if the owl were alerted to a noise from its movements against her cheek and hair. And if Cookie didn't hear her mother or her hungry brothers and sisters up in their nest, then maybe her mother would hear Cookie and her funny sounds. As if on cue, Cookie spoke.

Psssh-cheee. Psssh-cheee.

Callie walked past the tree stumps and deep into the wooded areas that hadn't yet been hacked down by King O' Corn. The trees were denser here, and hardly any moonlight made it through the foliage.

She felt nervous and lost, but Callie had made her mind up—she wasn't walking out again until she'd found the barn owls' nest.

Treetop Thrills

Looking up, Callie could just about see the moonlight on the leaves at the very tops of the trees, but at ground level, it was so dark she might as well have been wearing a blindfold.

She held out her arms in front of her, feeling for trees in the way, and placed her feet cautiously on the ground. Although she couldn't see, she noticed so much more, like the slightest puff of breeze on her face and twigs snapping underfoot. Rustles in the bushes made the hairs on her arms stand on end, but she knew it was probably nothing more than a squirrel or a mouse. Every now and then she stopped and held her breath, so that she and Cookie could listen carefully to their surroundings.

It seemed that there was nothing out there, and Callie wondered if she should think again—maybe she could find a friendly farmer who might know a rescue center for Cookie. But it was always better to keep a baby animal with its family if possible, and she was determined not to give up. She kept moving, as slowly as a sloth, reaching out for obstacles and stopping for sound checks. And then suddenly, she felt Cookie's head brush against her cheek as it swiveled.

Callie stopped. "I can't hear a thing, Cookie. Do you have an itch?"

But Cookie continued to rotate her head. She was trying to pinpoint the exact location of a noise. What noise? Callie could only hear the slight rustle of the bird by her ear.

Then Cookie shrieked. The sound was loud but squeaky, like sneakers on a smooth floor. *Scree-ee-ee.* Cookie had never made that sound before. From somewhere in the distance, a similar squeak came back—a high-pitched shrill. They were calling to each other.

"You clever girl, Cookie," Callie said. "I'd never have heard that if it were just me."

Cookie called again, and again the

call was returned.

"Got it," said Callie. "We're walking straight ahead, toward the sound."

Stepping carefully so she didn't fall, Callie made her way deeper into the woods. Every now and then, Cookie and the other owl exchanged cries, and Callie felt that they were getting closer. Closer to reuniting Cookie with her family.

High up in the canopy, caught in a smudge of faint moonlight, a huge white bird swooped down toward them before vanishing into the darkness.

Callie stood still, straining her eyes to see where it had gone, and Cookie sat quietly on her shoulder.

Out of nowhere, Callie felt a soft billow of air on her cheek, which she knew wasn't a Texas breeze. It was the bird.

"I think that's your mother," Callie said, feeling a chill of excitement.

The mother called from high in the treetops just as her wings caught the moonlight once again. Was she returning to a nest? Callie wasn't going to take her eyes off of the owl for one second.

Yes! She could just make out the mother landing on a branch and a hole in the tree trunk. A new nest, maybe. The beautiful owl hooted once again before ducking inside, and Cookie returned the call—*scree-ee-ee*. It was definitely her

mother! And even if the mother
owl hadn't been the best parent
in the animal kingdom, Callie
was determined to return her
baby to her.

Callie stood at the base of
the tree where the mother had
landed and realized it wasn't
going to be easy. With Cookie
still unable to fly, how was
she going to get her into
the nest? Callie didn't like
the idea of climbing all
the way up there.... But
what else could she do?
She ran her hands up and
down the trunk, feeling
for branches, but there
were none.

"What would an animal do?" Callie closed her eyes and pictured climbing animals, like monkeys and squirrels, imagining how they would solve such a problem. They would climb a nearby tree and swing across. Of course!

Callie felt around for a neighboring tree. She found it and reached up, managing to locate a branch. She could just about wrap her hands around it. The owl on her shoulder held tight as Callie pulled herself up, and then felt for the next rung of the tree ladder. She found one, then another and another. Luckily, this tree seemed fairly easy to climb—although doing it in the dark was going to be risky.

"Here we go, Cookie. If I slip, then we're both going to have to learn to fly. Fast!"

Cookie snuggled against her ear as if

she understood that Callie was nervous.
"I'm only joking. I know I can do it.
I've had to climb trees before, to rescue
animals or stay out of danger. I'm pretty
good at climbing, actually. The key is to
never look down."

Looking down was a terrible idea if
you were scared of heights, like Callie,
because it could make you dizzy. But
there was nothing to see but darkness
anyway, so Callie concentrated on the
light at the tops of the trees and kept
moving. She pulled herself farther up
the tree, taking her time. The tree trunk
narrowed the higher she went, and
Callie found it easier to wrap her arms
around it and hold herself securely. The
branches got closer together, too, so the
problem wasn't finding the next one to

move to, but rather avoiding bumping
her head or snagging her clothes—
things that might throw her off balance.

Eventually, she'd climbed so high that
she had reached moonlight. She was
far above the ground, and everything
below her feet was wrapped in darkness.
Her fear of heights melted away. At
that moment, all that mattered was the
pretty owlet on her shoulder and her
determination to get her home.

"So where is home?" she asked
Cookie. "It has to be around here
somewhere."

Scree-ee-ee. The sound was so loud, it
vibrated in her ear. But it didn't come
from Cookie.

It came from the owl next door.

Air Hop

Cookie shuffled impatiently, tickling Callie's cheek.

"I know we're close, Cookie," Callie said. "But please don't tickle me! I need to think."

Scree-ee-ee. Cookie screamed in her ear and stamped on her shoulder, making her giggle even more.

"I'll tell you what, if you're going to continue to be a wiggle-bottom, I'm going to need a safety harness."

Air Hop

Callie carefully pulled her cardigan from her waist and looped it around her back, tying the arms together on the other side of the tree trunk. Instantly she felt more relaxed and a lot safer. She pulled aside a thin branch, revealing the tree next to them. There were white feathers at the mouth of a hole. It had to be the nest! But even though it was in sight, it wasn't in reach, and Callie's plan to swing across like a monkey wasn't going to work.

"Oh, Cookie, it's no good," Callie wailed. "What are we going to do?"

She sat down on the perfect seat of a forking branch and sighed heavily. How was she going to get Cookie into her nest? She wanted to cry, but her vet's oath to help animals in danger stopped her. She had to go on—she *had* to!

There was nothing wrong with taking a break, though, so Callie allowed herself to relax and thought of good things to lift her mood. Like nature and how incredible it was that the animal kingdom lived on so many levels—from tunnels in the ground, to the thinnest twigs in the tops of trees. It was amazing, and who would have thought that she would be up here in the trees, seeing the world like a bird.

Just then, Callie noticed that the sky had lightened a little.

Unlike sunset with its rosy-golden tint, the dawn sun peeking over the horizon was as yellow as egg yolks, lighting the sky around it bright blue and picking out a few thin white clouds. Callie realized that she had the best seat in the house for this spectacle. Around her, other birds were waking up with little cheeps and flutters, and within hours, the woods would be awake with daylight animals. But not owls.

Feeling more positive, Callie petted the owl on her shoulder. "Time to get you to bed, Cookie. Should we try again?"

If she lay down on the branch and
spread her weight evenly, it might just
work. She untied her cardigan....

"Almost there," Callie said, edging along
slowly, her stomach churning with nerves.

Halfway along the branch, it started
to bend and shake. Callie considered
whether it would be safer to stand and
leap across like a squirrel, but her human
instincts held her back. Then the branch
dipped suddenly, and Callie shuffled
back to the safety of the tree trunk and

re-tied herself to the tree.

"It's no good, Cookie," she said. "I'll get you home. But we're going to have to climb back down and think of another way."

Cookie responded by hopping off her shoulder and all the way down her arm.

"Where are you going? No, Cookie!" Callie shrieked as the owl leaped off of her arm and onto the branch, moving farther along to where it thinned out. "What are you doing?"

Holding back her panic, Callie tried to coax Cookie toward her. If the owl were to fall, there was nothing she could do....

"Cookie, come on, little one."

To her relief, the owl turned and hopped back. She jumped onto Callie's hand and looked into her eyes. She tilted her heart-shaped face one way, then the other.

"What are you saying?" Callie said, sensing something strange in her little friend's behavior.

Then Cookie made a rasping sound and blinked slowly before moving back along the branch. Callie watched as the little owl spread her wings. She desperately wanted to crawl after Cookie and drag her to safety, but she knew that sometimes you have to trust nature.

Callie held her breath. The moment seemed to last forever, and then…. Flap! Cookie let go of the branch. She was flying!

Just a short air hop to the other tree, but she did it, landing perfectly.

"Yes, Cookie!" Callie cheered. "You amazing, wonderful little owl!"

Cookie was clearly proud of herself because she flew right back again, settling on Callie's shoulder, where she nuzzled her. Callie was certain that she could feel a cold little beak against her cheek, like a kiss.

"Don't get too confident now!" she laughed. "Although I'm glad you came back for a hug. This time, you need to go, and you need to stay."

Cookie spread her wings—white with light brown tips, as if she'd dipped them in chocolate milk. She twisted her head to look at Callie one last time and then flew.

Callie
watched
her go—just
one beat of
those splendid
wings, and
she was home.
Without hesitation,
Cookie ducked into the nest
hole.

"I hope they left some food for you,"
Callie said softly. "And I hope they
realize what a wonderful little owl you
are."

She wiped away a tear and looked out
over the woods. With her little feathered
friend safely back in her nest, surely it
was time for her to go home, too....

The Final Flight

With fingers of daylight creeping
through the branches, Callie could
now see how terrifyingly high she had
climbed. She had conquered situations
much harder than this, but she was
tired and a little heart-sore. Although
returning Cookie to safety had been
her goal, she was sad that their time
together was over.

"I'll just rest for a minute," she said
to herself.

Secured in her seat of branches, the cardigan tight around her like a harness, Callie took a moment to enjoy the sunrise. It was a magnificent sight, but she wanted to experience it with her other senses first, just as she had learned to do at night. The warmth, the smells, the sounds of life awakening.... She smiled and shut her eyes.

They had barely closed when her head felt as if it were spinning. Faster and faster. Was she falling? Had her cardigan come loose? Oh, no!

Callie's eyes flew open, and her heart leaped to her throat. She was in darkness, and she was spinning! She blinked, trying to figure out what was happening. Then there was a loud moan next to her. *Gabriel?*

"I feel sick," Gabriel muttered, one hand across his stomach, the other clinging to the safety bar.

Callie tipped her head back and laughed. She was back, still on the flying swings, flying as high as an eagle. Or an owl.

"It's not funny," groaned Gabriel.

Callie felt a rush of happiness. "Come on—stick your arms out like a bird. It feels wonderful!"

As the flying swings spun, Callie looked out past the town at the farms in the distance. It was still night, and the farm vehicles were heading home, their headlights dancing over the rocky farm tracks. She had a flashback of the combine harvesters, and a sense of unease nagged at her happiness.

"Are you feeling sick?" Gabriel gulped.

"No," Callie replied. "But I'll feel better when we're down on the ground."

"Me, too," said Gabriel. "I hate this ride."

Callie didn't hate the ride, but she'd remembered the King O' Corn Farm sign about clearing the trees. She had to contact the farmer and local animal groups to let them know about the barn owls. She had to do something. If not, then Cookie, her family, and all of the forest creatures would have nowhere to nest and hide.

The ride eventually ended, and Gabriel headed for the bathrooms, staggering as if he were on a boat in a storm.

"I'll wait here," said Callie, trying not to laugh.

Then someone called in a funny high voice. "Callie, Collie, Coo!" There was no mistaking who it was. Only her best friend, Ella, would shout out such a silly thing in front of a bunch of people. Ella ran at Callie and wrapped her arms around her in a huge hug. "Is your French friend still here?" she asked.

"Yes, but he's not feeling very well. We just went on the flying swings!"

"I love the flying swings. Will you go on them again with me? I'm here with my family, and my little brother is too small for anything but the teacups."

"I'm sorry, Ella. My parents are picking us up in a minute."

"Hang on, what's that? And *that*? And *that*!" Ella wrinkled her nose and plucked flakes of grass from Callie's top, and a pure-white feather that was sticking out from behind her ear.

"Where have you been, Callie?"

"On a Texas owl adventure!" Callie replied, just as Ella's dad arrived with Ella's very tired-looking brother.

"Oh, hello there, Callie! What have you been up to?"

"She's been on the Texas howl adventure!" Ella said. "Is that some new ghost train ride or something?"

Callie opened her mouth to correct her but decided it was probably better if she didn't have to explain. Besides, Ella had moved on and was now begging her dad for cotton candy. Eventually, he gave in.

"Hooray! See you soon, Callie Mallie!"

"'Bye, Ella," Callie laughed, shaking her head.

Gabriel appeared soon after, still looking wobbly, and they went to meet

Callie's parents for a ride back home.

Over a late-night snack, Callie and
Gabriel's parents listened to their stories
of the carnival—about huge cotton
candy and the ghost train, and, of
course, the flying swings. Gabriel told
everyone that it was *très amusant*. Callie
thought it was a lot of fun, too, and she
decided not to mention that actually
Gabriel had felt sick for most of the
ride.

"I flew like *un oiseau!*" Gabriel
exclaimed, making everyone laugh as he
swooped around the kitchen like a bird.
It reminded Callie of something she
needed to do.

She excused herself from the table and
went to the family computer, where she
composed and sent an e-mail to King O'

Corn Farm, telling them about the forest—how it was home to precious animals, including the magnificent barn owl. Then Callie found the flyers that Mr. Howell had handed out at school. There was a contact e-mail, and she wrote to him about her concern over land clearing in Texas. Mr. Howell must have been up late, tending to his owls, because he replied right away saying he knew owl rescue centers all over the country and

would alert them right away. Satisfied
that she'd done everything she could to
help her owl friends, Callie rejoined the
fun at the table, her heart light as a
feather.

Later, after they'd gotten ready for bed
and Gabriel had talked and talked and
then fallen fast asleep, Callie found
herself still wide awake. It had been such
an exciting time—having Gabriel's
family over to visit, going to the carnival
at night, the cotton candy and raspberry
slushies, the flying swings, and then …
finding herself in Skyville, Texas.

Her heart skipped as she remembered
the attack of the horned owl, the sight of
the giant harvesters, and the vicious
raccoon. But her heart fluttered most of
all when she remembered Cookie's

curious little face and the bond that she had made with the beautiful owlet.

On the other side of the room, Gabriel's gentle snoring reminded her of Cookie's funny noises. Worried that she would laugh out loud and wake him up, Callie looked for a distraction.

Outside the bedroom window, the night was velvet-black, and Callie pushed her nose against the glass to look at the full moon that hung like a mobile among the twinkling stars. Something caught her eye. A piece of paper on the wind?

No, it was a white bird. By the light of the moon, it appeared luminous, and Callie held her breath as she watched it glide closer, silent and graceful. A barn owl.

"Don't go," she whispered.

But it didn't fly past—it looped
upward and then dipped, then up again
before swooping down. It was making

a shape! Was it.... It couldn't be.... It was! It was a heart. Perfect, like a cookie cutter.

"High score for flying, Cookie!" whispered Callie. "You're an expert now!"

The owl stretched her wings and flew away, gliding like a feather on the surface of a pond, off into the night. This time, Callie was certain she was gone.

But then a squeak echoed from somewhere in the distant darkness. *Scree-ee-ee.*

"Good night to you too, Cookie," she said with a smile.

ABOUT THE AUTHOR

Rachel Delahaye was born in Australia but has lived in the UK since she was six years old. She studied linguistics and worked as a magazine writer and editor before becoming a children's author. She loves words and animals; when she can combine the two, she is very happy indeed! At home, Rachel loves to read, write, and watch wildlife documentaries. She loves to go walking in the woods. She also follows news about animal rights and the environment and hopes that one day the world will be a better home for all species, not just humans!

Rachel lives in the beautiful city of Bath, England, with her two lively children and a dog named Rocket.